poppie's adventures

SERPENTS IN PARADISE

Created by
Julie Yeh
&
Jack Hsu

The Islands of Hawaii

Historic Hawaii

Volcanic activity millions of years ago formed the beautiful Hawaiian Islands in the Pacific Ocean. TheHawaiian Islands were first settled by Polynesian explorers in the early part of the First Century. In 1778, British explorer Captain Cook "discovered" the Hawaiian Islands and named them the Sandwich Islands.

The Hawaiian Islands were united under King Kamehameha the Great in 1810. Subsequent events in history led to the elimination of the Kingdom and annexation of the Hawaiian Islands into the United States of American as its fiftieth state in 1959.

The major Islands of Hawaii are Oahu and the Islands of Maui, Kuai, the Big Island (Hawaii), Molokai, and Lanai.

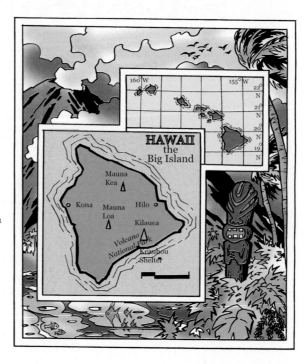

The Volcano and the Legend of Pele

The Big Island, Hawaii's southernmost island, is still in the process of being formed by volcanic activity. Its still active volcano, Kilauea, constantly pumps out lava, attracting tourists to the incredible sight at Hawaii's Volcanic National Park. Kilauea is the home of Pele, the Hawaiian goddess of the volcano. Legend has it that volcanic eruptions on Hawaii are the results of an angry Pele.

Hawaii's Animals

Much of Hawaii's plants and animals were brought to the islands as people started to settle there. Many animals that thrive in other parts of the world are not native to Hawaii. There are no snakes indigenous to the islands, and in fear that unwanted snakes would destroy some of the existing animal species in Hawaii and thereby upset the delicate ecological balance of the Islands, the Hawaiian government tries hard to prevent snakes from arriving on the islands. The few that can be found are under eradication programs.

"Poppie Field"

Poppie, age 17, is a talented young woman who decides to take some time off from her first year in college to experience the working world.

She lives with her cat, Mr. Tidbits, on a house boat in Sausalito, California.

After weeks of searching, she manages to land her first job with the San Francisco based magazine "The Young Traveler" as a junior writer.

James "Ham" Hamamura

Ham is a photographer at "The Young Traveler". He is a devotee of outdoor activities and enjoys rough and tumble sports.

He teams up with Poppie to cover vacationing in Hawaii. While Poppie aims to rest and relax during her trip, Ham has other ideas.

To Daughters Eileen and Chloe

Poppie's Adventures ⓒ Serpents in Paradise ⓒ
Story by Julie Yeh
Art by Jack Hsu

Published by Way Out Comics
P.O. Box 642218, Los Angeles, CA 90064
email:julieyeh@sbcglobal.net

Printed by Brenner Printing Company
First Printing, June 2003

McGregor! This strike is dragging on way too long. I'm completely broke. The union better negotiate faster or I'll have to cross the picket line.

You gotta hang on a little longer for better wages Bernie. Listen. I got a two week gig to transfer some cargo to Hawaii on my deep sea fishing troller, *"The Riveter"*...

...I'm not to ask any questions about the cargo, but I was promised that it doesn't contain drugs or weapons. The pay is fantastic. Help me out and I'll make it worth your while...

These poor men. It's hard to make ends meet when you're out of a job. I was in the same boat just yesterday.

Cool, Mr. Wendell! You're sending me to Hawaii for my first assignment?

That's right, Poppie. I'd like to have you and photographer James Hamamura do an article on vacationing on the Big Island.

You're leaving in two weeks. Here's your itinerary. You'll like James, ...

He's an excellent photographer and a real gentleman.

Great! I'll get started on my prep work and research.

Boy! Look at this rain! Good thing I'm prepared.

AHHH!

The Staff of
Kebechet.

Kebechet is the Egyptian goddess
who symbolized the purification by
water in the funeral cult.
Kebechet is personified by the
giant snake, who is the protector of
the pharaohs in death.

It is possible that the worshiping
of the snake goddess was in some
ways associated with the rebirth,
or renewal of life for the pharaohs, and
the Staff of Kebechet was believed
to have powers of resurrecting the
dead, as well as the power to attract
snakes of all kinds.

The cult of Kebechet has virtually
disappeared in modern cultures,
as snakes have been actively
hunted and destroyed around the
world, unable to find a sanctuary in
which they can thrive.

To Keauhou Shelter, please.

I guess Ron decided to ditch us... Still, gotta get Ham out of there before anything bad happens.

Oh no! The place is deserted. Where is Ham?

That boat over there. It must be "The Riveter"

Let's see if there is any activity on the boat.

Ham!

Poppie! **Help!** Get me out of here!

I have some snake repellent with me, but I don't know if it works . . .

Guess there's no better way to find out. Ugh!

It works! It works! Hurry Poppie! Hurry!

Trust me. I'm going as fast as I dare!

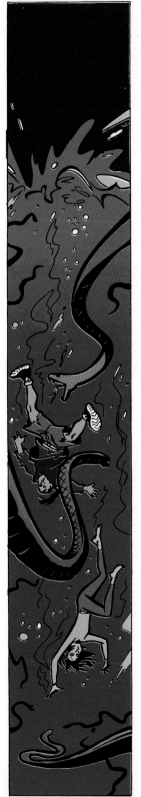

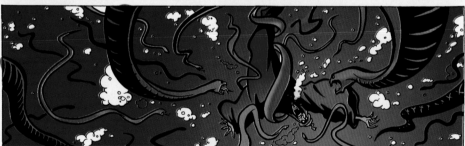

How did you manage to find us Ron? I couldn't find you at the police station.

Perfect timing man! Thank you! Thank you! Thank you!

Well, the police didn't believe me at first and sent me packing . . .

. . . then these two gentlemen showed up with their story and led the police here.

We're so sorry! We had no idea . . .

Attention! This is Hawaii 5-0. You are under arrest!

Two weeks later, back in San Francisco.

Bravo! Bravo! Isn't it heavenly, Ham?

Huh? Wha....?

Well, I guess it's back to the office tomorrow.

I just hope Mr. Wendell likes what I wrote.

You know, after losing most of my photos in the caves, I wish we can do the Hawaiian assignment again . . .

" . . . except this time, I hope we won't encounter serpent worshipers who want to revive the snake cult again."

the making of *Serpents in Paradise*

1. Night time: Poppy is at Kapa'a'a Point. She looks around
with her binoculars and thinks to herself:
          "Hmmm. I know I have forgotten to do something ealier
           and I can't remember what it is to save my life! Any way
           I'd better find Ham ASAP."
Poppy sees Ham's jacket on the beach.
          Poppy: (Thinking)
           " Why is Ham's jacket lying over there?"
2. She looks around and sees Ham's bandana with blood stains.
          "Oh no. That's Ham's Bandana! Those cult members must
           have caught Ham. He must be in serious trouble."

3. Looking from behind a volcanic rock with binoculars towards
the sea. Shadow of a fishing troller is anchored in the distance.

4. Binocular view: fishing troller with the name "Navigatress"
and a headboard featuring a curvaceous woman wearing a sailor's
hat. Light shines through the window.

          Poppy: (thinking)
           "That's it! The Navigatress! I wonder if Ham is on
            board the boat."

5. Poppy takes off her clothes. She has a bathing suit
underneath.

6. Poppy puts on flippers.
          "Anyway there is only one way to find that out. I've got
           to save him if he is in trouble."

7. Poppy swims towards the boat. She carries her clothes in a
waterproof backpack. She suddenly remembers what she had forgotten.
          "Darn! Now I remember what it is that I forgot: tell Ron
           about the Navigatress. I guess I have to try to go it
           alone now."
8. Poppy climbs up the ladder leading up to the boat deck,
looking at her watch.
          "It's almost midnight. I hope I'm not too late."

9. Sees three large crates at the back of the boat. Small
aerosol cans are next to the crates.
          Thinks:
           "Ugh. Those longshoremen are right. These crates do
            stink badly! It must be the snakes."

10. Poppy picks up one of the cannisters. On it are the words
"snake repellent."

11. Poppy sprays some of the repellent on her body.
          Thinks:
           "Huh! Not nearly as fragrant as my perfume, but I guess
            I'd better use some of it. Can't tell whether I'll
            stumble onto one of those nasty creatures again."

12. Poppy peeks through the window of one of the lighted cabins.
          Poppy:
           "Ham!! Oh No!"

13. Inside, we see Ham standing on a chair. Two large snakes
guarding him, and he is sweating.

          Poppy:
           "Psst. Ham!"

14. Close up of Ham, staring straight at the snakes.
          Ham (whispering):
           "Poppy. Hellp!!!! Get me out of here!!"

15. Poppy tosses one of the canisters of snake repellent to Ham.
          Poppy:
           "Catch, Ham. Spray it on yourself and at the snakes.
            See if it helps."

16. Ham directs the spray at the two venomous snakes. They recoil
and turn away from him.
          Ham (still shivering):
           "It's working. Thank god. I thought I was going to
            become snake dinner."
          Poppy:
           "Are you hurt, Ham? I saw your jacket on shore with some
            blood stains on it."
          Ham:
           "I'm O.K. I got a few cuts when I fell off a
rock in the cave. That's how I got caught. Anyhow we've
            gotta stop those madmen before they ruin this island."
          Poppy:
           "Unfortunately I forgot to tell Ron about this boat, and
            he and the police are probably searching for you on shore
            right now. Looks like it's up to us to stop the
            cultists."

17. Ham and Poppy climbing out of the cabin.
          Ham:
           "We've got to hurry. I overheard that they are going to
            let the snakes swim for Hawaii from the ocean in
            accordance to some ancient tradition in order to revive
            their cult."

18. Ham and Poppy sneaks toward the back of the boat. They see
several of the cultists open the crates. The serpent master (Ika
Re) is standing higher up, with the staff raised above his head.
One of his followers is dumping the snakes from the last of the
crates. Several empty crates are strewn about the deck.

          Ham (Look of horror on his face):

           "Oh no!!! We're too late. The snakes are loose."

The Origins of *Poppie's Adventures*.

The original idea of *Poppie's Adventures* came about during our first trip to the Big Island where we had the chance to visit the Kilauea volcano at Hawaii's Volcano National Park, and were introduced to the legend of Pele.

For our first comic book, we wanted to create something that is suitable for younger readers, and wanted to stay awayfrom the superhero genre. We also decided that we wanted to have our storylines driven by the history, culture, and geography of different countries and places in the world. Finally, after having two daughters, we decided to have the main character for this book be a young woman, and her side-kick friend, an Asian American. Thus came the idea of Poppie and Ham.

Future books in the Poppie series will include World War II history in the Roman ruins of North Africa, and a culinary mystery in Paris.

The Creators

Julie majored in English literature at Wellesley College, and has some other post graduate degrees in miscellaneous fields. She occasionally writes for fun.

Jack Hsu was professionally trained as an architect at Yale University, and is currently an illustrator for films such as Spiderman II, and The Haunted Mansion.

Both Julie and Jack grew up outside the United States: Julie in North Africa, and Jack in Taiwan and Japan. Some of the inspirations for this book include *The Adventures of Tintin, Asterix*, and the works of Hayao Miyazaki.

Acknowledgments

We'd like to thank the following people who've given us helpful tips throughout our journey to get this book published: Romi Cummings from Wellesley College, Susan from Digital Room, Ming Tai, Sindy, Ivy, Andy, our daughters whom we tested the storyline to on several occasions, our parents, Donna Barr, Cindy Roberds and Wayne Cartwright from Brenner Printing, Trina Robbins and Anne Blaeske from Friends of Lulu, Steve Leaf from Diamond, and of course, the Xeric Foundation.

Contact Us:

Way Out Comics
P.O. Box 642218
Los Angeles, CA 90064

email: julieyeh@sbcglobal.net
        jack.hsu@sbcglobal.net

Our websites, poppiesadventures.com and wayoutcomics.com will also be up and running, so please check there for information on future comic book products.

This book is made possible by a generous grant from the Xeric Foundation.